FAMILY KARATE

FAMILY KARATE

KATHRYN EWING

BOYDS MILLS PRESS
CAROLINE HOUSE

Text copyright © 1992 by Kathryn Ewing
Illustrations copyright © 1992 by Boyds Mills Press

All rights reserved
Published by Caroline House
Boyds Mills Press, Inc.
A Highlights Company
910 Church Street
Honesdale, Pennsylvania 18431

Publisher Cataloging-in-Publication Data
Ewing, Kathryn.
    Family karate / by Kathryn Ewing.—1st ed.
[96] p. ; cm.
Summary: Jennifer Conlan is thirteen, and life at home is like one big karate match.
So she writes a letter to an advice column in her favorite teen magazine, but the
answer is not what she wanted to hear.
ISBN 1-56397-117-8
1. Family life—Juvenile fiction. [1. Family life—Fiction. 2. Brothers and sisters—
Fiction.] I. Title.
        [F]—dc20   1992
Library of Congress Catalog Card Number: 92-70088
First edition, 1992
Book designed by Tim Gillner
Interior illustrations by Judith Hunt
The text of this book is set in 13-point Palatino.
Distributed by St. Martin's Press
Printed in the United States of America
10 9 8 7 6 5 4 3 2 1

To Jessica who made a suggestion,
and
to Dana, who made a correction,
and
to Jean, friend of a lifetime

–K.E.

Chapter One

I never expected "Dear Denise" to answer my letter. I just wrote it and mailed it off to *Totally Teens* "Problem Corner" one day when I got disgusted with my whole family and couldn't think of anything better to do.

Dear Denise,

My problem is my family. I am thirteen. I have an older sister, who is eighteen; a brother, seventeen; a little brother, eight years old, and a little sister, six. We fight all the time, especially at the dinner table. And then our parents get mad and start fighting, too. I'd really like to change this. What can I do?

Signed: Tired of Family Karate

I never expect anything to really happen when I do something crazy like this. I forgot I wrote that letter until today, when I find *Totally Teens* waiting for me on top of our old upright piano, together with all the other magazines and junk mail our family gets. Right away I open it to "Problem Corner," and there it is: my letter! My very own words in black print on a smooth white page, and looking so good I think for a minute that maybe some other kid has the same problem I have.

From outside I can hear those two little twerps, my sister Emily and my brother Robert, arguing down by the swing under the maple tree in the backyard; and I know that within minutes it will sink into their pea brains that I have arrived home and been delivered into their hands to be tortured for the rest of the afternoon.

Therefore, I take *Totally Teens* and sneak up to my bedroom on the third floor, being careful to avoid all creaking boards in the stairs of this big old Victorian house my parents are so thrilled about living in. Not that Emily and Robert can hear me from way down in the backyard, but just because I try to keep a low profile in this family. I am a naturally quiet person, a thoughtful person, a future poet (I hope!). I need peace and quiet in order to think, and I live in this house where there is *never* any peace or quiet, and most of the time people don't think at all.

Anyway, I creep up the stairs to my bedroom

on the third floor. Living with four siblings (*siblings* is what Sister Kristie Anne, my eighth grade teacher at Holy Redeemer Catholic Elementary School, calls brothers and sisters), I would go bananas if I couldn't escape to this little room my father framed in for me in our attic and shut the door.

So here I am, looking down at my magazine spread out on my bed, and here is my letter looking up at me. My letter. The first writing of mine ever to appear in print! And here is Dear Denise's answer to it:

Dear Tired,

Fights among siblings are part of growing up, but it sounds to me as though things at your house are getting out of hand. When disagreements arise, try putting yourself in your brothers' and sisters' shoes (and your mom's and dad's, too). Seeing things from someone else's point of view can go a long way toward defusing an argument. And don't forget that 'a soft answer turneth away wrath.' Try this and see if you won't all have a lot more of those special good times that only big families can share.

Right away I read the whole thing over again five times. Well, all right, I read the *Dear Tired* part two times and my *Dear Denise* part five times. My words look so much more important in print!

Anyway, I am starting from the beginning again when I hear Emily come banging up the stairs, calling my name and crying. Em is such a whiner. I don't know how my parents stand her. They say they love us all equally, but how can anyone be equal about a whiner like Em?

Bang, bang. My door doesn't have a lock, but my parents have this rule that nobody can open a closed bedroom door without being invited to do so. (An excellent rule, I must say.)

So bang, bang again.

"Whaaat?" I shout.

Emily cries harder and tries to talk at the same time, so all I get is: "Jen . . . Jen . . . Jen . . . hiccup, hiccup ugh oo Robert beep po yump bump, Jenifuuuurrr."

"Whaaat?" I shout again. But I don't want to hear all those ughs and yumps again, so I say, "Come . . . in!" Em comes in, and her uniform has got dirt all down the front of it.

At Catholic school we have to wear uniforms every day. By the time spring rolls around, I almost can't stand to put on a white blouse and blue plaid jumper one more time. I do put it on, of course. And from grade one I have understood that as soon as I come home I change my clothes, so my uniform won't get

dirty. Emily knows this, too.

"What happened to your uniform?" I say.

"Rob . . . ert," she begins, opening her mouth so wide I can practically see her tonsils.

"Not Robert," I snap. "Not Robert. Emily. How did Emily get dirt all over her uniform?"

Hiccup, hiccup. "Waldo . . . pushed . . ."

"Not Waldo!" With Emily, someone else is always to blame—even Waldo, our big, goofy part-Airedale mutt.

Hiccup, hiccup. "The swing . . ."

"Not the swing! You weren't supposed to be on the swing in your uniform."

For a long time I stare at her. Coldly. The way our gym teacher, Mrs. Fleming, stares at us eighth grade girls if we try to get out of gym class.

Emily's lower lip trembles. Her face looks like it's going to break apart. She looks pathetic. And she knows it. She gives this look to our parents, and they fall for it every time. But I don't.

"Jennifuuurrr. . ."

I hate it when she calls me this. "Not JenniFUUURRR!" I tease.

She throws herself onto the floor. "Oh, you won't help me. You aren't taking care of me. You're supposed to take care of me until they get home."

By "they," Emily is referring to our parents.

My mom, Mary Conlan, is office manager at Wilbur Container Corporation, Inc., in Twin Forks, and my father, Theodore Conlan, is a lawyer right here in town. Except for Thursdays, when Mrs. Seeley comes to clean and I go for my piano lesson, I am in charge of Emily and Robert from the time I get home from school until "they" get home from work about five-thirty or quarter to six. For this, I am paid a small weekly salary.

As my parents have more than once pointed out, the only way we can live in this big old Victorian house, the only way we can have the things we need and want, is for everyone to put a shoulder to the wheel. My sister Mary Lou didn't want to go to college, so when she graduated from high school last year, she got a job as receptionist at Home Owners Real Estate, and she pays room and board. Michael is a senior at Hamilton High, and he works at Pauley's Garage after school and on Saturdays to help save for college. I think I have the hardest job of all, stuck with Emily and Robert.

Emily now has stopped crying and is curled up on the floor, whimpering to herself. It's not fake this time. She sounds as though she's going to just lie there on the old hooked rug covering the dusty floor of my room and fall asleep. My eye catches Dear Denise's letter. "Try putting yourself in your sisters' and brothers' shoes . . ."

I flop down on the floor beside Em and brush back the wisps of blonde hair plastered against her forehead. It's damp with perspiration, but how silky fine it is.

"Are you tired, Emmy?" I ask softly.

She looks up at me as if she thinks I'm playing some sort of trick on her. I feel awful. I mean, putting myself in Emily's shoes, how can this little kid bear to have someone like me shout and yell at her every day after school? I'm mortified.

"Hey, look, Em," I say. "How about I change my clothes, and then we'll go down and change your clothes and wash your face off with nice cool water. And then we'll go outside and sit on the porch swing, and I'll read you a story. Would you like that?"

She looks astonished at this kindly suggestion.

"Would you like that, Em?"

She decides to trust me. She smiles. A front tooth is missing. How would I like to be this little kid, only in first grade, with all she's got to learn about nouns and verbs and catechism still ahead of her? How would I like to be six years old again? How would I like to have *me* for a baby-sitter? As I said, I'm mortified.

Before we go out to the front porch swing, we

go down to the kitchen and I set out milk and cookies for Emily and Robert. I get an apple for myself, because I have started this program not to fill up on junk food.

I call Robert in from the backyard where he has been twirling around on the swing, scuffling his feet in the loose dirt and kicking up a lot of dust. I don't yell at him about this because I can see he has changed from the dark blue pants and white shirt and tie that boys have to wear to Catholic school, and has put on a T-shirt and a pair of jeans. I never have to remind Robert about things like this, because Robert is Mister Perfect, and prides himself on doing everything just right.

"I want to tell you what Em did," he says as soon as he opens the back screen door.

I am scrubbing off the potatoes we're going to have for supper and putting them into a pot. This has to come before reading to Em. "Don't be a tattletale," I tell him.

Robert scowls. "If you know something of importance, something of importance that a certain person has done that is wrong, you are supposed . . . *supposed* . . . to tell it. Like if you knew someone was planning to murder someone, then you are morally bound . . . *morally bound. . .* to go to the police and tell on that person."

This brother of mine is only eight years old, but he is never wrong.

I say, "I don't think Emily is planning on murdering anyone."

Emily giggles. I smile at her. We are on good terms.

Robert stuffs a Fig Newton into his mouth. He takes a swig of milk. A white mustache appears on his upper lip, which he wipes off with the back of his hand; then he wipes the back of his hand on the back of his pants. "Em took dirt and rubbed it on the front of her uniform," he says. "De-lib-er-ate-ly."

Emily chokes, spits milk, then bursts into tears. "No! Oh, no! No! No! Oh, I didn't! I didn't! I didn't!"

"Like this," says Robert. He reaches down and mimes picking up earth and plastering the front of his shirt with it.

"Oh, no! No, no no!" wails Emily.

"You see what you've done?" I demand of him.

Robert's eyes widen. "Me? Me? She did it! She! That's not fair! You're not fair! I'm going to tell them as soon as they get home. I'm going to tell them on you, Jen."

I run water from the spigot over the potatoes and set the pot aside. "Tattletale," I say.

"Tat—tle—tale," Emily sings. "Tat—tle—tale."

I wish she wouldn't. It occurs to me that if I were in Robert's shoes, I'd say I was unfair, too. He runs out, slamming the screen door.

I look at Emily. "Emily, why did you rub dirt on your uniform?"

Emily claps her hands over her ears and squeezes her eyes shut. "Oh, you'll punish me, you'll punish me!"

"Emily . . . ," I begin quietly.

"You'll punish me, you'll punish me!" she screams.

"I won't punish you!" I scream back. (So much for the soft answer that turneth away wrath.) "Now tell me!"

"Because," she moans, "I'm sick, sick, sick of that old blue plaid uniform."

I sigh. I can see that blue plaid uniform from Emily's point of view perfectly. "I'll sponge the dirt off and press it," I tell her.

She beams. I feel her soft little hand slip into mine. "I love you, Jennifer," she says.

She has never said this to me before. (Not that I blame her.) But what surprises me is how happy her words make me. She loves me! This little kid loves me! I give her hand a squeeze.

Dear Denise, Could it be you're a genius?

Chapter Two

Reading a story to Emily isn't the only reason I want to be on our front porch. The other reason—okay, the real reason—is because Brandon Ackerman (also in the eighth grade at Holy Redeemer School) delivers our *Times Herald* newspaper. Sometimes I arrange to be sweeping our front walk as he passes by. Sometimes I am raking dead leaves out from under our rhododendron.

Sometimes, I admit, I am standing at our living room window, watching up the street for when he comes tooling along on his bicycle to sail a newspaper up onto the Haldemans' porch three doors down. Then I rush outside and begin calling for Emily and Robert, even though I know they are inside the house or playing in the backyard. And when Brandon pulls up to the curb, I'm right there ready to run down our front walk and take our newspaper from him, giving us a chance to talk.

"Here comes Brandon," Emily shouts.

My heart skids as I see him head toward our house, taking a newspaper form his sack.

"I'll get it!" she chirps.

"*I'll* get it!" I mutter, and dump her storybook into her lap. "Look at the pictures," I command, and hurry down to the curb.

Brandon hands me our newspaper. "Hi," he says.

"Hi," I say.

"So how are things?"

I heave a big sigh, as if I'm burdened. "Right now I'm reading Em a story."

He smiles. (That smile! I'm like to die!) "What story?"

"*The Lion, the Witch & the Wardrobe.*"

"Hey, I read that once. I liked it."

"Em likes it." (I'm not sure she really does, but I want to keep the conversation going.)

"Well . . .," he says.

"Well . . .," I say.

"Are you going to the Paradise this Saturday?"

(The Paradise is the big roller skating rink out by the new shopping center.)

"I think so," I say.

"I hope so," he says.

Right that second, I *know* so, but I say, "I'm going to call Cara Gialilli tonight and see if she's going."

"If she goes, then are you going?"

"I guess so."

He smiles again. "I hope so."

"Why? Are you going?"

"Maybe. If you're going to be there . . . ."

"Oh," I say. But I can't believe he has said this! I can't believe I got so lucky. When he wheels off, I run back up the walk, throw my arms around Emily, and kiss her.

Chapter Three

My life is relatively peaceful until around five-thirty each afternoon, when my parents and my sister Mary Lou and my brother Michael troop home.

Until then, I am occupied with taking care of Robert and Emily, practicing my piano lesson, doing my homework, taking care of Robert and Emily, setting the table for supper, and taking care of Robert and Emily. At five o'clock, Robert and Emily get to look at television, and I get to talk to my friend Cara Gialilli on the telephone.

This afternoon I tell her, "Brandon Ackerman stopped to talk to me."

Cara knows that Brandon has been stopping to talk to me almost every afternoon for three weeks. But she understands this is worthy of mention because she knows how much Brandon means to me.

"What did he say?" she asks.

"I think he's getting to like me a little."

"I'm sure he's getting to like you. A *lot*."

Cara makes me feel good, the way only a best friend can.

"Guess what?" she says. "I got asked to go to our graduation dance."

Cara makes me feel bad, the way only a best friend can.

"That's great!" I tell her. "Who asked you?"

"J.J. Hernandez."

I don't happen to think J.J. is all that wonderful, but at least she got asked.

Our eighth grade graduation dance is in two weeks. It's the last dance of the school year, and the only dance where boys ask girls, and everybody really gets dressed up. If you don't get asked by a boy, you can go with a bunch of girls, the same as to our other dances. But I say a prayer that Brandon will ask me!

Cara says, "Brandon is going to ask you to go with him, I bet."

I say, "Oh, thank you, Cara. Thank you for saying that!"

"I'm making a novena," Cara says. "First, I was making it for my intention, but now that I've been asked, I'm making it for yours."

"Oh, thank you!"

Making a novena for someone else's intention is really, really nice, because a novena is a lot of special prayers that you say every day for nine days. If you forget to say them for even one day, you have to start all the way back at the beginning and say them all over again.

While I'm thanking Cara, my brother Michael comes into the hallway where our telephone is. He is gross with grease from working at Pauley's Garage all afternoon. "Get off the phone," he says. "I have to make a phone call."

"So?" I say.

"So get off the phone."

"I am talking to my friend, and—"

I don't get to finish this sentence. Michael whips the telephone out of my hand. "She'll call you back," he barks into it. Then he starts punching buttons.

"Michael!" I shriek. "I was talking on that telephone!"

"Shut up!" he shouts. "I gotta work tonight. I gotta break a date with Amy right away."

I make a pass for the telephone. "Give me back that phone!"

Into the telephone Michael says, sweet as pie, "Hello, Mrs. Lipp. Is Amy—"

I press a button and cut him off.

"Jennifer!" he yelps.

"What in the world is happening?" It's Mom, home from being office manager at Wilbur Container Corporation, Inc.

"I was talking on the telephone," I screech.

"And Michael came in and—"

"Mom, I gotta work tonight!" Michael shouts. "I can't go to Amy's concert at the high school, and Jennifer wouldn't hang up so I could—"

"Wouldn't hang up! You didn't ask, you just barged in."

"Mom!" It's Robert. "Emily rubbed dirt on the front of her uniform! Like this!" He does his wiping-dirt-on-shirt routine. Sometimes Robert can be the twerp of the twerpiest.

Emily darts out from behind him and throws her arms around Mom's knees. "Oh, don't listen, don't listen, don't listen! Oh, no, no, no!"

Waldo starts barking and jumping around.

The front door swings open. "I come home to this?" It's Mary Lou, the family actress, home from being a receptionist. "This?"

"Knock—it—off!" It's my father, home from being a lawyer. Fath can shout louder than anybody.

In the sudden silence, I find myself remembering Dear Denise. "Emily and I have discussed what she did to her uniform," I say quietly. "She's very sorry, and I've sponged it off and pressed it."

My family stares at me as if they're caught in a freeze-frame. I look at Michael and connect with the long white florist's box he has put on the telephone table. It really doesn't take much imagination to figure out how he must be feeling.

"Michael," I say, "I'm sorry you have to miss out on Amy's concert tonight. Maybe Mary Lou and I can go and sort of represent you, give Amy your flowers afterwards. Okay, Mary Lou?"

"What?" says Mary Lou.

"You and I take Michael's flowers to Amy at the high school tonight, okay?"

Mary Lou flings back her head and frowns at

the ceiling, then says, "I might as well. Friday night, and nothing else to do."

Last year Mary Lou was voted the most popular girl in Hamilton High's senior class. She played the lead in her senior play. She was even queen of the Thanksgiving football weekend. But now all her old friends are away at college, and I don't honestly think she's tried to make new ones.

Before my letter to "Dear Denise," I might have snapped out something like, "Well, whose fault is it if you don't have something to do?" Instead, I say, "This time last year, you had jillions of dates beating down the door. I know that all your friends are away at school."

Mary Lou looks at me as if she can't believe anybody remembers how sought after and popular she once was, as if she's going to burst into tears.

I feel as if I'm going to burst into tears, too.

Dear Denise, Maybe I'm too emotional to put myself into other people's shoes.

Chapter Four

I love Hamilton, the town where we live. It's an old town, with big old trees and old houses that have been kept up and streets with wide pavements, some of them still brick or slate. On Sunday mornings you can hear church bells ringing all over town.

Walking along to Amy's concert at the high school, Mary Lou is grumbling about how hot and humid it is. It is May.

"My hair is kinking up," she says.

Mary Lou has pale blonde curly hair that is prone to kink. I don't mean kink pretty. I mean just kink.

I look at her. "You look beautiful," I tell her.

This is absolutely true. Even with kinky hair, Mary Lou is beautiful. I've always observed this, especially as I'm not beautiful. I look like a regular person: kind of watery blue eyes and drab brown hair. But Mary Lou is beautiful (although before "Dear Denise" I would never have told her this).

"Beautiful, ha!" says Mary Lou.

"You are."

"Stop trying to antagonize me."

"Antagonize you!" (We've picked up words like this from our father, the lawyer.) "But it's true."

"Nobody thinks I'm beautiful. Nobody likes me or thinks anything about me at all. And if you don't stop antagonizing me, I'm going home."

"You can't go home," I tell her. "Michael is counting on us to deliver his flowers to Amy after the concert."

"I don't care."

"Try putting yourself in Michael's shoes."

Mary Lou studies me through narrowed eyes. "Something is going on with you. You've changed."

"Changed?"

"Yes, changed."

"Changed how?"

"I'm not sure."

"For the better?" I ask hopefully

"Maybe," says Mary Lou.

Dear Denise, Is this progress or what!

When we get to the high school, cars are turning into the parking lot and people are rushing into the auditorium, many of them carrying bouquets and boxes of flowers.

Inside the lobby, a gentleman approaches us.

"Good evening, Jennifer," he says.

The gentleman is wearing a suit and tie, so it takes me a minute to recognize him as John Mitchem, usually dressed in clothes appropriate to being my brother Robert's new soccer coach. When I figure out who he is, I, too, say "Good evening," although normally I'd just say, "Hi, Mitch."

Mitch is looking at Mary Lou now, and I remember my manners. "This is my sister, Mary Louise." (Somehow, it seems right to be formal.) I turn to Mary Lou. "Mary Louise, this is Mr. John Mitchem."

Mary Lou holds out her hand. If you weren't related to her, you wouldn't know her face doesn't always feature this darling blush of pink.)

"How do you do," Mary Lou breathes.

Mitch bows over her hand, and I get this mental image of Sir Walter Raleigh and Queen Elizabeth.

"My pleasure," he says.

He has a deep, wonderful voice. This surprises me, because I've only heard him shouting at all those little kids on the soccer field.

"Thank you," murmurs Mary Lou.

Mary Lou doesn't sound exactly like herself, either.

Then the lights start flickering on and off, and we have to hurry to take our seats.

"Who is he?" whispers Mary Lou as we settle down.

"Robert's new soccer coach," I whisper back.

"Is he married?"

"Shhh!" somebody from behind us hisses.

I scrunch down in my seat. I don't know if Mitch is married, but I'm going to find out.

Chapter Five

Saturday morning is absolutely my favorite time of the whole week. On Saturday mornings I don't have to take care of Robert and Emily; I don't have to get up early to go to church and, of course, I don't have to go to school.

From downstairs comes the noise of my family. But up here in my little attic room I can spend the whole morning reading or writing in my diary or just sitting at my window looking down at our pear tree, thinking about—not much of anything. I love my room. I *love* it!

But the morning after Mary Lou and I go to Amy's concert (we told her she was very good and she cried with happiness over Michael's flowers), I am out of bed and down the stairs to the kitchen bright and early.

"Look who's here!" Fath says. He is at the stove, making his famous scrambled-eggs-with-capers Saturday morning breakfast for himself and Mom. He claps his hands: *clap, clap, clap,* like it's a miracle I made it out of bed.

"You're down early," Mom says. She's working through the family's outdated notes, clippings, and appointment reminders plastered over the double doors of our refrigerator.

Mary Lou doesn't say anything. She's standing at the clothes dryer folding the wash. (At our house somebody is always folding wash.)

"Where's Robert?" I say.

"Need you ask?" says Mom.

I go out to the sun porch, and there are Robert and Emily, in their pj's, feeding their brains to the TV set.

I wait until a disgusting canine halitosis commercial comes on, then lower the volume.

"Hey!" Robert yells.

"Just for a minute," I say.

"We love that commercial!" Emily says.

I ignore this. "Robert," I say, "is Mitch married?"

"Huh?" says Robert.

"Mitch, klunkhead. John Mitchem. The guy who teaches all you little twerps how to kick a soccer ball. Is he married?"

"No," says Robert.

"How do you know he's not?"

"Michael told me."

"*Our* Michael?"

"Michael tunes up his car."

Well, well!

"You are a very useful boy," I tell Robert. I pat the top of his head, turn up the volume on the TV set, and leave the room.

Mary Lou has disappeared from the kitchen. Another load of wash is spinning in the clothes dryer. Mom and Fath are eating at the big round table in the center of the kitchen.

"Mom," I say, "if Mary Lou and I do all the work, could Michael ask John Mitchem to come to dinner?"

"Robert's new soccer coach, John Mitchem?"

With all she has to do and think about, it amazes me how my mom keeps up on things!

"Why would you want Michael to ask Robert's coach to dinner?" My-father-the-lawyer is speaking.

"Because," I say, "he's Michael's friend and a very nice person, and Mary Lou met him last night, and he happens to be unmarried, and. . ."

Quick as a wink, Mom says, "I'll ask Michael to call John."

She smiles at my father. My father smiles at her. They both smile at me.

Even though my parents love all five of us siblings equally, sometimes, just for a while, you can get to be their favorite. Right now, I know I'm my parents' favorite child.

Thank you, Dear Denise!

Chapter Six

The Paradise Roller Skating Rink is located out at the Covered Bridge Shopping Center, and that's where Mary Lou drops Cara Gialilli and me off this Saturday afternoon.

When she drops us off, Mary Lou does not say, "You kids have got three hours, and you'd better be standing outside when I come back because I'm not waiting for you."

No, indeed!

She says, "What time would you like to be picked up?" She actually smiles when she says this.

When we climb out of her little car (I'll be so glad when I can drive), she even tells us to have fun.

As she drives off, she waves her hand!

My friend Cara, who knows Mary Lou very well, asks, "What's with Mary Lou all of a sudden?"

"There's a man in her life," I answer.

Mom has spoken to Michael, who has called John Mitchem, who has accepted an invitation to come to dinner at our house next Sunday at twelve o'clock noon. I tell this to Cara.

"It figures," she says.

Best friends always understand.

The Paradise Roller Skating Rink is huge. On Saturdays a lot of little kids celebrate their birthdays here, and so now parents are hurrying in with birthday cakes and balloons, taking them upstairs where there are long tables that kids can sit at and eat ice cream and have their birthdays without making a whole lot of extra work at home.

Downstairs, music is playing over the PA system and it's kind of dark, with yellowish lights spreading a golden glow over the rink. Kids are circling around on their skates, the little kids sticking close to the railings at the sides and the older kids out in the center. Some of the older kids get really fancy with their dance steps, but I like to just drift along with the music.

Today, however, as soon as Cara and I rent our skates and put them on, I look for Brandon.

"Do you see him anywhere?" Cara whispers to me. We have moved out to the edge of the floor, and she is swiveling her head all around.

"Cara, please don't do that with your head," I beg. "He'll see us looking for him."

"You mean, he's here!" Cara exclaims, her eyes large and dark. "Where? Where is he?"

"Please, Cara!"

"Well, is he here?"

"I don't think so."

"I'll skate around. If I see him, shall I tell him you're looking for him?"

"Yes," I say. And then, "No!" And then, "Oh, I don't knowwwww!"

Cara suddenly points a finger out at the center of the floor. "There he is, there he is, there he is!" she squeals.

I ask, "Where? Where?"

Cara drops her arm. "False alarm."

I'm like *dying*! "Cara, please do not do that again."

"I'm sorry, Jennifer. I really thought—" She stares over my shoulder. Her eyes bug out, and she grips my arm. As if she's strangling, she says, "It sfim!"

I say, "Whaaat?"

"It sfim, it sfim, it sfim!"

"Hi, Jennifer," says a voice behind me.

I turn.

IT SFIM.

Chapter Seven

Dear Diary,

I have never been so happy in my life! This afternoon I went to the Paradise Skating Rink with Cara. Brandon Ackerman was there, and we skated together all afternoon. We held hands while we skated, and sometimes he put his arm around me. He said he would never let me fall down. He is so—oh— oh wonderful!!! I am the luckiest girl in the world.

P.S. I think he might ask me to our eighth grade graduation dance.

After I finish writing this, I go downstairs to telephone Cara from what used to be a pantry until my father was made a partner in his law firm and needed an office-away-from-the-office for all the extra work he brings home.

It is Saturday night. My parents have gone to

a benefit dinner at the Hamilton Country Club. Michael has a date with Amy (naturally), and Emily and Robert are tucked into their little beds. I use my father's office telephone because Mary Lou has finished doing her nails and is looking through a book of recipes in the living room, which is too near the hall telephone for any privacy whatsoever.

I open the window by my father's desk and take a deep breath of the soft night air. It smells of earth and flowering trees and springtime. It smells heavenly. Then I dial the Kemptons', where Cara is baby-sitting.

"Are they asleep?" I ask when she answers, meaning Buster and Penelope, the Kemptons' two little kids.

"Yes," says Cara.

I take a bite out of a Fudgie-Fudgie. Since being with Brandon all afternoon, I'm like crazy!

"So what do you think?" I say.

Cara doesn't beat around the bush. "I think he really likes you."

"Do you really?"

"Didn't he tell you?"

"Tell me what?"

"That he likes you."

"No, he didn't."

"Well, anyone could tell."

"Oh, Cara, do you really think so?"

"He skated with you all afternoon."

"Yes, but . . ."

"And probably the only reason he came was because you said you were probably going to be there."

"Yes, but . . ."

"He's sure to ask you to our graduation dance."

"Well, I don't know. . . ."

"Or you could call and ask him."

I don't say anything right here, because I know Cara could do something like this, but I never could!

Cara says, "I noticed he had his arm around you a lot of the time this afternoon when you were skating. That means he cares."

Streaks shoot through me. "Oh, Cara, thank you for saying that!"

"Well, I really think so."

"Oh, Cara, thank you!"

I would love to keep on talking like this, but I'm so excited I have to hang up and go to the bathroom, which is in what used to be a large coat closet in our front hallway.

When I come out, Mary Lou calls me into the living room.

"I want to read you the dinner menu for next Sunday," she says. "Actually, I have two menus here."

She rummages among sheets of paper scattered over the design of green pine trees and brown pinecones on our sofa. "The first is: salad, steak, twice-baked potatoes, and cherry pie topped with vanilla ice cream. How's that?"

I'm having a hard time getting my mind off Brandon. "Sounds good," I tell her.

"You like the idea of twice-baked?"

"Twice-baked?"

"Weren't you listening?"

"Run it past me again."

This time I listen, and I get scared. "Do you know how to fix those potatoes?"

"There's a recipe right here in this book," Mary Lou says. "They sound yummy."

"Let's hear the second menu," I tell her.

"A vegetarian dinner: twice-baked potatoes, spinach souffle, creamed celery, and cranberry flan."

I can see she has fixated (Father's word) on those twice-baked potatoes. But creamed celery? Spinach souffle? Cranberry flan?

"Mary Lou, I promised Mom that you and I would do all the work, don't forget. Including the cooking. Also, how do you know if Mitch is a vegetarian?"

This simple question gets my sister hysterical.

"Jen—ni—fer!" she shrieks, "I've been sitting here all night wracking my brain trying to make this dinner perfect, and you are throwing obstacles up to everything I say!"

I do not believe this! Yes, I do! Oh, Dear Denise . . .

"Mary Lou," I say, "let's you and me figure out how we want the table to look, and ask Mom to help us figure out what to put on it."

Mary Lou frowns at myriad sheets of paper scattered over green pine trees and brown pinecones. She gives a sigh of relief. "Good idea."

Dear Denise, Take a bow!

Chapter Eight

In my experience, the people who say all good things must come to an end are right.

Consider Sunday. It's raining, but that's okay. I love rain, especially a nice steady drizzle that slides off the roof and falls into puddles under our clogged gutters with soft, friendly plops.

This day starts off fine, with my brother Robert, all polished up for church, knocking at my bedroom door.

"Jennifer," he says when I invite him in, "I appreciate the way you fixed it with Mom so Mitch can come for dinner next Sunday. It was very nice of you."

Some people might feel it incumbent (Father's word) to explain to Robert that he has had nothing whatever to do with the reason John Mitchem is coming to the Conlan house for dinner next Sunday at twelve o'clock noon. But in a large family, you tend to get blamed for things that are not your fault, so whenever I'm given credit, I take it. "You're very welcome, Robert," I say.

"It was magnanimous." (Father has a profound influence on all of us.)

"No problem," I say.

He smiles. He has a sweet smile. There may be hope for Robert.

But is there hope for the Conlan family on this rainy Sunday?

No!

Because Mr. and Mrs. Theodore Conlan are not speaking to one another. They are not looking at one another. They are not having anything to do with one another. The five Conlan children know without being told that Mr. and Mrs. Conlan have had a fight. Mr. and Mrs. Conlan's fights are silent fights. Their children hate this worse than their own loud fights.

Their children hate it while sitting in the Conlan van during the silent ride to Mass. They hate it while sitting in Holy Redeemer Church, with Mr. and Mrs. Conlan at either end of the pew and the five Conlan children between them, instead of sitting side by side, as they normally do. Their children especially hate it after Mass, when they go to King's Deli for their usual treat of Sunday morning brunch, because it is very embarrassing to be in a restaurant with your parents when:

1. They are not speaking to one another.
2. They do not smile at the waitress.
3. Your mom says, "Nothing but coffee. Black."
4. Your father groans—out loud.
5. Nobody else at the table says anything.
6. It takes a long time for the waitress to bring your order.
7. It's so quiet you can hear everybody chewing.
8. Your father doesn't touch his bacon and eggs.
9. Your mother sips her coffee and looks out the window.
10. Your little brother says, "Mom, I don't feel so good."
11. Your little sister says, "Mom, Robert says he doesn't feel so good."
12. Your mom says, "He'll be home soon."
13. Your father says, "Oh, this is fun. Fun, fun."

It's a situation even Dear Denise couldn't deal with.

Or could she?

As soon as we get home, I sprint up to the third floor, pull *Totally Teens* from under the sweaters in my sweater drawer, and open it to "Problem Corner." Then I run back down to the second floor, shove it under the door of my parents' bedroom, and wait!

Would you believe that, fixing supper in the kitchen tonight, my parents are speaking to one another?

They do not look at one another. They do not smile. But they are speaking.

After supper, when Mary Lou and I are in the kitchen loading the dishwasher, we hear Fath start playing the piano. We love the times when he plays the piano. We finish up fast and hurry into the living room.

Amy and Michael are already there, sitting on the pine tree and pinecone sofa, holding hands. Amy is at our house a lot. Michael has been dating her since they got to liking one another in the eighth grade. I wonder if this will happen to Brandon and me. Eek!

Father is playing "I'm Poor Little Buttercup," from Gilbert and Sullivan's *Pinafore*. Mom always sings this song. It's her song, you might say. She sings it now, but she doesn't look at my father. She sings it to the picture of two deer that hangs above our fireplace.

When it's over, we all applaud and Mom drops a curtsey. Then Fath plays "Poor Wandering One," from *The Pirates of Penzance*, and Amy sings. Amy has a beautiful soprano voice; and then Michael sings "A Policeman's Life Is Not a Happy One." After this, Amy, Michael, Mary Lou, and I sing "When I, Good

Friends, Was Called to the Bar" and "A Wand'ring Minstrel," and last of all, "Tit-Willow."

By this time Emily is in Mom's lap, swinging one foot, her thumb stuck in her mouth. She's too old for this, but when she's tired, she still does it. And Mom and Fath are looking at one another—finally!

Robert is not singing. Robert never sings. Robert listens. He closes his eyes and listens with his whole body. He seems to be drawing the music into him through his nose. Fath says Robert possesses greater musicality (*his* word) than anyone in our family.

We sing the last verse of "Tit-Willow" very softly. Fath puts his finger to his lips, and we get softer and softer, letting the song die out: "Oh, willow, tit-willow, tit-willowwwww."

When it's over, nobody moves. We all look at Robert. Robert opens his eyes. "Like angels," he says.

We burst out laughing and applaud ourselves.

Later, when I'm upstairs doing homework, there is a tap at my door. It's my mom, and she has my *Totally Teens* in hand. I get shaky inside. I don't know if she's mad about me sticking it under their bedroom door. But all she says is, "You and your pen pal write good letters."

When she goes downstairs, I hear her and my father laughing.

What can I say?

Dear Denise, You're incredible!

Chapter Nine

I would like to be able to report that the success of my Dear Denise strategy with my parents is a good omen for the week ahead.

Alas, I cannot.

It rains on Monday. It rains on Tuesday. It rains on Wednesday. I do love rain, but this is ridiculous!

On the blackboard in our eighth grade classroom, Sister Kristie Anne writes:

Rough winds do shake the darling buds of May.
From the "Sonnets"—Wm. Shakespeare

I love this quotation. I copy it into my notebook. Each day, on my way to and from school, I gaze into yards filled with dripping azalea bushes, wind-tossed pink and white dogwood petals, and dear little pale green leaves spinning like whirligigs on the maple trees.

Rough winds do shake the darling buds of May.

"How true!" I mutter.

But that's not all.

Each day Brandon Ackerman delivers our *Times Herald* wearing a yellow slicker, his hair plastered down on his head. Rainwater runs into his eyes, drips off his chin. He does not look happy. Although I stand in the living room, saying Hail Marys and ready to wave to him, my prayers are not answered. He does not look up.

Each day Emily stands at the window beside me and says:

1. What are you doing?
2. Why are you looking out the window?
3. Are you looking for Brandon?
4. Why are you looking for Brandon?

Each evening over the telephone, my best friend Cara says:

1. Did Brandon come by?
2. Did you speak to him?
3. Why not?
4. You could call him. Are you going to call him?

On Thursday it's cloudy and cold. I take my piano lesson. But on Friday, the sun comes out, and Sister Kristie Anne writes on the blackboard:

For, lo, the winter is past,
the rain is over and gone;
The flowers appear on the earth; the
time of the singing of birds is come,

and the voice of the turtle is heard
in our land.

"Song of Solomon"—The Holy Bible

I love this quotation! I copy it into my notebook. But that's not all!

This afternoon Emily and Robert are in the backyard, pulling weeds out of Mom's vegetable garden. I have arranged to be right down by the street, taking my time shoveling up the dirt and stones that the rains have washed down our driveway and onto the pavement when along comes Brandon Ackerman. He wheels up to our curb and holds out our *Times Herald* to me. When I reach for it, he quickly switches it under his arm and catches my hand.

He is holding my hand! I can't *believe* this is happening to me!

He says, "Lot of rain."

"Yes," I say.

"Have you ever been to a kite fly?"

"No." I hold my breath. He is going to ask me to go to one!

"It's out at Pebble Creek Park," he says. "J.J.'s parents are going. They're taking J.J. and Cara. J.J. says they'll take us, too. If you want to go, that is."

"Sure."

A date with Brandon Ackerman!

He lets go of my hand. He has been holding it all this time. He gives me our *Times Herald*. "Okay," he says. "I'll come by for you on Sunday around noon."

"Sunday? Around noon?"

Oh!

Ohhhhh!

Ohhhhhhhhh! No!

Brandon looks at me kind of funny. I think this is because I'm looking at him kind of funny. "What's the matter?"

"I can't go on Sunday," I say. "We're having a guest for dinner. I promised to help out."

"Oh," Brandon says. "Okay."

He shoves off. I watch him wheel past Schultzes' house next door. The Schultzes don't take the *Times Herald*. I watch him toss a newspaper onto the Keelers' front lawn. I watch him turn the corner into Harvey Street and disappear.

I am devastated.

Devastated.

Dev—as—ta—ted!

Chapter Ten

It is three minutes later, and I have called my best friend Cara on the telephone.

"I don't believe this!" she shouts into my ear. "I don't believe you are *real!*"

"Well, what could I do?" It's very hard for me to speak these words because of the tears in my eyes and the lump in my throat.

Being my best friend, Cara is merciless. "You could have said yes! That's what you could have done. You could have said, 'Thank you very much, Brandon. I'd love to go to the kite fly with you and Cara and J.J. on Sunday.'"

"But I promised to help out with Coach Mitchem's dinner!"

"You could have gotten out of that."

"I couldn't! I gave my word!"

"You could have gotten out of it! You could have explained things to your mother. She would understand."

"Not when I gave my word."

"She would. Any mother would."

"I don't think so. And, anyway, Mary Lou is counting on me."

"Mary Lou would understand."

"Mary Lou would never understand."

Being acquainted with Mary Lou, Cara says, "Well . . ." Then she says, "Well, Mary Lou has never been very nice to you, don't forget."

This is true. Until very recently (like this week) Mary Lou has never been nice to me at all. But is this a reason to go back on my word?

"So?" I say.

Cara loses her cool. "So, forget the kite fly!" she shouts. "Forget the kite fly! Forget Brandon Ackerman!"

She hangs up!

I hang up!

But I will never forget the kite fly.

I will *never* forget Brandon Ackerman.

Chapter Eleven

It is the next day, Saturday, and I am sitting at my window gazing out at my pear tree on which little lime green pears are nestled among darker, leathery-looking leaves. I am not, however, thinking about pears. I am doing a Dear Denise, trying to put myself into Brandon Ackerman's shoes.

Myself: "If I were Brandon Ackerman, how would I feel if Jennifer Conlan said she couldn't go to the kite fly with me?"

Brandon's shoes: "First of all, Brandon really wanted Jennifer Conlan to go to the kite fly with him. Remember that."

Myself: "I know, I know! That makes me so happy! But then, when I said I couldn't go. . . I mean, will he ever ask me anywhere again?"

Brandon's shoes: "Put it this way: Why wouldn't he?"

Myself: "Oh, I don't *knowwww!*"

Brandon's shoes: "Look, analyze it. When he delivers newspapers, doesn't he always stop to speak to you?"

Myself: "Almost always."

Brandon's shoes: "Do you believe he stops to speak to every girl he sees?"

Myself: "Well, no."

Brandon's shoes: "And he held your hand, don't forget."

Myself: "I could never forget that!"

Brandon's shoes: "And anyway, don't you just know in your heart he cares?"

Myself: "Yes!"

Brandon's shoes: "So?"

I smile and blow a kiss to the little green pears on the pear tree.

As I go downstairs, I can hear from the sun porch that Emily and Robert have the volume turned up on their Saturday cartoons. I can hear that Fath is on his tractor, mowing the front lawn. Michael, I know, will already be off to his job at Pauley's Garage. That accounts for almost everybody.

"Where's Mom?" I ask Mary Lou, whom I find in the kitchen.

"Planting her impatiens."

Mom is the gardener of the family. Each spring she plants a border of salmon pink impatiens in front of the juniper bushes around our front porch.

Mary Lou opens the door to the fridge. "Want some O.J.?" she asks, taking a carton of orange juice from the shelf.

Mary Lou? Pouring my orange juice? I scarcely have strength to raise my glass to my lips.

"I'm ready whenever you are," she says brightly.

The kitchen table is loaded with Mom's blue and white wedding china, with Grandmother Conlan's sterling silver that we inherited, and with Great-aunt Harriet's crystal stemware that we got the same way.

We haven't used any of this finery (Mom's word) since Mom got a job at the Wilbur Container Corporation, Inc. Even before that, we used it only on Christmas and Easter, or when my parents gave a dinner party. But Mom has agreed to let Mary Lou use it now, if we polish the silver and wash (by hand) the china and stemware that have been collecting dust in the corner cupboard of the dining room.

I try to estimate how long it will take Mary Lou and me to do all this.

"Where would you like to start?" my sister inquires politely.

I remind myself that it was my idea to invite Coach Mitchem to dinner. I swallow my orange juice. "Mary Lou, where would *you* like to start?" I ask.

Two hours later, we have run out of silver polish and the hot, sudsy dishwater has pleated the skin on my fingers like the inside of a mushroom cap. But I have to admit that the dining room table, with our best white tablecloth on it and with Mom's pretty china and Gram's sterling silver and Aunt Harriet's stemware, looks just the way Mary Lou wants it to look: perfect.

Fath looks in from mowing the lawn and says, "Wow!"

Mom looks in from planting her impatiens and says, "Lovely!"

Robert and Emily say, "Grueful!" (*Gruesome* plus *beautiful*: Robert's word.)

Mary Lou and I stand around admiring the effect we have created. Then I grab two Fudgie-Fudgies, and we get into Mary Lou's neat little car and hie ourselves to the Covered Bridge Shopping Center.

Only one problem: By this time on a Saturday Cara and I would have spoken to one another on the telephone at least twice. Today we haven't

spoken at all. She has not called me; I have not called her.

This is the WORST thing that has EVER happened to me!

It's even worse than not getting to go to the kite fly with Brandon Ackerman. Cara and I have been best friends since first grade. Nobody in the whole world will ever take Cara's place. And we are not speaking!

As I push a basket around the Shop 'n' Save, following Mary Lou and her menu, I try not to think about it. I help choose apples and avocados for Mary Lou's salad of apples and avocados with honey mustard dressing. I help select potatoes for her twice-baked potatoes. I form an opinion on the best-looking leg of lamb. (Mom has suggested roast leg of lamb. If Coach Mitchem turns out to be a vegetarian, he can have an extra twice-baked potato.)

In the evening I keep praying for our telephone to ring and for it to be Cara, calling me from the Kemptons', where she baby-sits on Saturday nights. I keep saying Hail Marys for this to happen, so we can get back to normal and be best friends again.

Our house is quiet for a change. Fath and Mom have gone to visit friends. Michael has a date with Amy (naturally). Mary Lou is upstairs in the bathroom shaving her legs so she will be perfect for tomorrow, her big day. Robert and Emily are sound asleep in their little beds.

I go into Father's office-away-from-the-office, stare at his telephone, and do a Dear Denise:

If I were in Cara's shoes, wouldn't I be sorry I had banged down the telephone and hung up on my best friend?

If I were in Cara's shoes, wouldn't I be too ashamed to call me up and apologize for such rude behavior?

If I were in Cara's shoes, wouldn't I be sitting at the Kemptons', praying their telephone would ring, and that it would be me?

Of course I would!

Then why don't I do this?

BE—CAUSE I NO LON—GER FEEL LIKE PUT—TING MY—SELF IN SOME—BODY ELSE'S SHOES!

Chapter Twelve

The next day Coach John Mitchem eats some of everything, including *two* of Mary Lou's twice-baked potatoes.

That night, around seven o'clock, Cara calls me. I am not expecting anyone to call me, so I'm very surprised when I pick up the telephone and it's Cara.

"Cara!" I say.

Cara says, "So how was the big dinner party?" (She sounds a little remote.)

I say, "Fine! Everything turned out fine!"

"How did our beautiful heroine make out with her hero?"

"I think they've fallen in love."

"Hmmm."

"I really think so. She told me he asked if he could call her, and she said yes."

"Great."

I change the subject. "So how was the kite fly?"

"Brandon came with us."

"He did?"

"And Sharon Riley."

I'm not sure what I say right here. Maybe I don't say anything, because Cara says again, "Brandon came with us. And Sharon Riley."

I say, "Cara, I heard you the first time."

Suddenly, Cara is shouting. "Jennifer, you make me so mad! We could have had so much fun! And you can tell Mary Lou for me that I hope she is very, very happy because, thanks to her stupid dinner party, Brandon Ackerman has asked Sharon Riley to our graduation dance!"

"So?"

I do not know how I manage to speak this word, for my heart is breaking.

"So you have no one to take you to our graduation dance!"

"So!" It's the only word I can think of.

"So forget our graduation dance! Forget you aren't going!"

She hangs up!

I hang up!

But how can I forget our graduation dance?

How can I forget I'm not going?

Chapter Thirteen

It is Monday morning. I am sitting in the eighth grade classroom on the second floor of Holy Redeemer Elementary School on Maple Avenue in Hamilton, Pennsylvania. I am copying the poetry that Sister Kristie Anne has written on the blackboard:

The year's at the spring
And day's at the morn;
Morning's at seven;
The hillside's dew-pearled;
The lark's on the wing;
The snail's on the thorn;
God's in his heaven—
All's right with the world.
                "Pippa's Song" from *Pippa Passes*
                —Robert Browning

Sister Kristie Anne says, "This poem is often misquoted. You'll sometimes hear, 'God's in his heaven—All's *well* with the world.' However, Mr. Browning was not such an optimist as to tell us that *all* in this world is well."

How true!

This morning I do not look at Brandon Ackerman. I do not look at my best friend, Cara Gialilli.

At lunchtime I hurry down to the lunchroom and sit between Elyse DeStefano and Rachel Henderson. After lunch I am standing in the school yard with Rachel and Elyse when Cara comes up and asks if she can speak to me. We walk a little away from the others, and Cara says, "I want to apologize for the two times I hung up on you on the telephone. I was upset. I just felt so bad about you and Brandon."

Isn't Cara nice? I mean, she may have a temper, but I love her so much! She's the best friend I'll ever have. I don't know why I have to go and spoil everything.

"I don't care to discuss it," I say.

"Right, *ri-ight*," Cara says, as if she doesn't notice how snippy I am. "Why care about somebody who would turn around and do what Brandon Ackerman did? I mean, asking Sharon just because you were loyal and kept your word to your sister. You know what I mean?"

"I don't care to discuss it," I say again.

(Sometimes my mom says this to Fath, and right now it's all I can think of.)

"Anyway," Cara says, "J.J. says he can get you a date for our graduation dance."

Inside my head it's like lights turn on—flashing red, flashing blue, flashing yellow; like I'm a police car on an emergency, with sirens screaming. "Nobody has to get me a date for our graduation dance! I don't want to go to our graduation dance!"

"Is that what you want me to tell J.J.?" (Cara is beginning to lose her cool.)

"Yes!"

"I think that's dumb."

"So?"

"So I think it's dumb, that's all!"

I watch Cara whirl around and walk away. Why do I have to be like this? Why can't I call her back, apologize, do something? I'm letting my best friend walk away.

I'm breaking my own heart!

That afternoon Brandon Ackerman sails by on his bicycle and throws the *Times Herald* onto our front walk without even looking up.

I know he doesn't look up, because I have

been watching for him from behind the pine tree and pinecone draperies in our living room. Does Brandon even remember that as recently as three days ago he was holding my hand?

"There goes Brandon! There goes Brandon! There goes Brandon!" Emily shouts, jumping up and down.

"I don't care," I tell her.

"Then why were you watching out the window for him?"

"I was not watching out the window for him."

"I bet!"

Emily is young, but she isn't stupid.

That night I do not call Cara. Nor does Cara call me.

After supper Mom takes Emily upstairs to give her a bath. At the kitchen table Fath slaps together tomorrow's school lunches (sandwiches: bologna, with mayo, for Emily and Robert; bologna, with mustard, for Michael; bologna, with a little mustard and a little mayo, for me).

At the dining room table Robert gets started on his homework. From the turnaround in the driveway Michael backs out his car and heads for the library—to research a paper, he tells us (as though all of us Conlans don't know he will stop by Amy's house on his way back home).

Mary Lou and I load the dishwasher. Then Mary Lou goes into the dining room to check Robert's homework, and I put a leash on Waldo to take him out for his evening walk.

Doesn't everything at the Conlan house seem peaceful? No more fighting, shouting, crying, stamping up and down stairs? Not even a dog barking?

Can all this be the result of my letter to Dear Denise?

Of course it can!

Consider:

Because Mary Lou makes Michael happy by delivering his flowers to Amy, Michael makes Mary Lou happy by inviting Coach John Mitchem to dinner, which makes John Mitchum happy to invite Mary Lou to a movie, which impresses Robert into letting Mary Lou look over his homework, all of which makes my mom and fath happy because there is no more fighting, shouting, crying, and stamping up and down stairs, which makes Emily (who is not stupid) look around the table at suppertime and say in surprise, "Everybody's happy!"

And everybody IS. Except me, of course.

When I get home from walking Waldo, I go up to my room and shut the door. I'm so grateful for this little room of my own! It's a very small room. Because of the eaves, the ceiling slopes down like a tent, so you can stand up straight only in the center of it; and the window is so low that, to look out, you have to squat on the floor. But I love my room with all my heart.

And I never get tired of looking out at my pear tree. It's so beautiful in the moonlight. When the tree is filled with blossoms, it looks like a ballet dancer all in white. In winter it reminds me of a very old lady, the way its bare branches are twisted and bent, the bark running along each gnarled little twig like veins in old hands. But when the snow comes whispering down to cover it, its loveliness breaks my heart.

I curl up at my window now and look out at my tree. It helps me to forget about things: the graduation dance, Brandon Ackerman, even Cara. A wisp of cloud floats like a scarf across the face of the moon.

God's in his heaven—
All's right with the world.

Chapter Fourteen

Tuesday after lunch I do not stand in the school yard talking to Elyse and Rachel. I do not stand in the school yard on Wednesday, either. I go upstairs to our eighth grade classroom and ask Sister Kristie Anne if I can help her change the water in the bouquets of flowers on our May altar.

In Catholic schools, during the month of May, a small altar is sometimes set up in a corner of a classroom to honor the Blessed Virgin Mary, who we believe is the mother of Jesus. This altar is just a table on which is placed a statue of the Virgin, together with some old jelly and peanut-butter jars filled with lilacs, tulips, pansies— whatever the kids bring in.

At Holy Redeemer it's usually the lower grades downstairs that set up May altars. But Sister Kristie Anne loves May altars, so we have one, too. You can smell lilacs and lilies of the valley as soon as you get to our door.

Sister Kristie Anne doesn't ask any questions when I come in from the school yard on Tuesday, but by Wednesday, she has picked up on something.

"What are you doing up here again?" she says.

"I've come to help you with the flowers," I tell her.

Sister Kristie Anne raises one eyebrow. (I've practiced raising one eyebrow. Hard to do.) "I hear," she says, "that you aren't going to your graduation dance because Brandon Ackerman has asked Sharon Riley."

I say, "Who told you that? Cara Gialilli?"

This makes me so mad. I mean, telling Sister Kristie Anne all about Brandon Ackerman and me . . . !

Sister says, "I know someone who would be happy to escort you."

I am furious! I say, "*No one* has to escort me. I do not want to go. And I shall never speak to Cara Gialilli again!"

Sister Kristie Anne says, "I think that's dumb."

She scoops up a vase of lilacs and carries it off to change the water at the sink in the Girls' Room down the hall.

The next day, which is Thursday, she writes on the blackboard:

I was angry with my friend:
I told my wrath, my wrath did end.
I was angry with my foe:
I told it not, my wrath did grow.
            "Songs of Experience"—Wm. Blake

I do not—repeat, not—copy this quotation into my notebook.

On Thursday, as usual, Mrs. Seeley comes to our house to clean, and to keep an eye on Emily and Robert while I go for my piano lesson.

Alison Houston is my piano teacher, and I take my lesson in her home. Her little boy, Toddie, is only six months old, and if he starts fussing, I pick him up after my lesson and take him out to the Houstons' kitchen to feed him orange juice while Alison teaches Lawrence Rimmer, who has his lesson right after mine. (Lawrence Rimmer happens to also be in the eighth grade at Holy Redeemer Elementary School.)

Alison says she keeps one eye on Toddie and two ears on whoever is playing the piano. Today, my playing isn't worth two ears.

"What's the matter?" Alison asks gently, after I have failed to flat the same B for the third time. Beside me on the piano bench, she touches my arm. "Is your concentration just off today?"

I attempt a careless shrug, but the loving

kindness in Alison's deep blue eyes blows me away. The inside of my nose prickles, I can't swallow, and my eyes fill up with tears.

"Jennifer!" Alison gasps. "What's the matter!"

"I don't have a date for my graduation dance!"

Alison's face turns crimson. She throws her arms around me. "Oh, Jen—ni—fer!" she wails,

and bursts into tears. "That happened to me, too! I know just how you feel!"

Seeing his mother cry, Toddie starts to scream his head off. Alison hauls him onto her lap, clutching him in one arm and putting her free arm around my shaking shoulders. "Oh, Jennifer, Jennifer, Jennifer!"

We are now all three blubbering into each others' faces. This whole scene suddenly strikes me as so hysterically funny that I start to laugh. I can't stop. I laugh and laugh. I gasp for breath. Each time I look at Alison's sad face, I laugh harder. Alison looks sadder, and Toddie cries louder.

It is at this moment that Lawrence Rimmer, music book in hand, arrives for his piano lesson.

That night I answer the telephone. It's Alison. "Jennifer, I have a date for you for your graduation dance."

"Thanks, Alison," I say. "But I don't want to go."

"Jennifer, listen to me . . . ."

"Alison, I *don't* want to go. Thank you very much, but I don't want to go. Period." (When I'm mad, I sound icy cold, just like my mom when she's mad.)

Alison sighs. "Ho-kay."

I get off the phone, and my mom looks in from the living room. "What was all that about, Jennifer?"

I wish there was more privacy in this house. "It was just Alison Houston."

"And . . . ?"

"She just wanted to say she could get me a date for that stupid graduation dance."

"But didn't I hear you tell her you don't want to go?"

"Yes, ma'am."

"Why in the world not?"

"Because," I explode, "I don't happen to like Alison Houston and Cara Gialilli and J.J. Hernandez and Sister Kristie Anne scrounging around trying to get dates for me!"

Mom looks at me, and I can practically see inside her head where things are spinning and clicking. Then she says, "I wonder what your pen pal would have to say about that?"

She doesn't elaborate, but this morning when I wake up, I find this sheet of yellow paper from one of my father's legal pads shoved under the door.

I read: *If you can put yourself into other people's shoes, how come other people can't put themselves into yours?*

I look down at my pear tree and think about this. I will concede (Father's word) that Mom has a point here.

BUT I DON'T WANT OTHER PEOPLE PUTTING THEMSELVES INTO MY SHOES!

Chapter Fifteen

During this exciting week of the graduation dance, for almost the entire eighth grade of Holy Redeemer Elementary School, nothing else of any importance is happening in the town of Hamilton or in the United States of America or in the world.

Elyse DeStefano asks me if I want to go to the dance with her and Rachel Henderson. They don't have dates and are planning to go together. I say no, thank you. Then Rachel Henderson asks me the same thing. My answer: ditto, Rachel.

I do not speak to Cara Gialilli. When I see her, I look down at the ground or up at the sky.

Not speaking to Cara is the hardest thing I have ever done in my whole life.

On the blackboard Sister Kristie Anne writes:

The quality of mercy is not strained
It droppeth as the gentle rain from heaven
Upon the earth beneath. It is twice blessed
It blesses him that gives and him that takes . . .
The Merchant of Venice—Wm. Shakespeare

I say this over to myself. It is so beautiful. Then I copy it into my notebook.

While I'm doing this, Sister Kristie Anne is saying, "Why do you suppose Shakespeare says, 'It blesses him that takes?' We can understand why it is thought a blessing to give. But might there be times when taking is the difficult thing to do? Are there times when we refuse to let others help us? When we refuse to give others the chance to show their generosity and love? Can this be what is meant by false pride?"

Sister Kristie Anne raises one eyebrow and looks at me.

Are my mom and Sister Kristie Anne on the same wave length or what?

At home I baby-sit Emily and Robert each afternoon. I practice my piano lesson. I eat Fudgie-Fudgies.

My family knows that Brandon Ackerman

does not stop by to talk to me, because Emily has told them he does not stop by to talk to me.

My family knows I am not speaking to my best friend, Cara Gialilli, because I am never on the telephone speaking to Cara Gialilli.

My family knows I am not going to my graduation dance, BECAUSE THERE IS NO PRIVACY IN THE CONLAN HOUSEHOLD AND EVERYBODY KNOWS EVERYTHING ABOUT EVERYTHING!

On Wednesday night Mary Lou taps at my bedroom door.

"I was just thinking," she says, "maybe you'd like to go to a movie with Johnnie and me on Friday night."

She calls him Johnnie now. *Some* people make progress.

"Thanks, but I don't think so," I tell her.

"Jennifer, I know how you feel."

"Nobody can possibly know how I feel."

"Try me."

I turn and look out the window at my pear tree.

After supper on Thursday night I harness up Waldo for his evening amble. Michael follows me out the back door.

"I'm taking Amy to the fire company carnival over in Twin Forks tomorrow night," he says, loping along beside me. "Want to come?"

"Thanks, but I've got plans for tomorrow night," I snap.

"What plans? Sitting up in your room looking out at the pear tree?"

He turns and goes back home. I've hurt his feelings.

I'm a monster.

I know I am!

When I go to bed, I can't sleep. I toss and turn. Maybe it's on account of getting my period. Maybe it's on account of being a monster. When I finally do fall asleep, I have wild dreams. They wake me up, and I go and sit at my open window and lean my head against the frame.

There is no moon. The night air is heavy; nothing stirs. All up and down our street, lights are out in every house. In our house, too— except for the light downstairs in the old pantry, my father's office-away-from-the-office. I can see the light from this room streaming out across the yard.

I look at my clock. It's after one.

Suddenly, I'm scared. My father works so hard, so long, so much! Has something happened to him, all alone down there?

A silent scream streaks through me. I jump up and race in my bare feet down the two flights of stairs, through the living room, the dining room, the kitchen. I fling open the old pantry door without knocking. My father looks up from his desk. "Why, Jennifer! What's the matter?"

I am weak with relief, with happiness. I cannot move. Tears fill my eyes.

"I thought . . . when I saw your light . . . it's so late. I was afraid. . . ."

"Why, Jen," he says. He gets up and comes to me and puts his arms around me. "I'm fine. Just fine."

He rests his chin on the top of my head, and we stand this way. Then he says, "How about a glass of milk?"

So we have a glass of milk, just the two of us. My feet are freezing, but I don't care. I shall never care about anything dumb again. I shall never care about missing out on a stupid graduation dance. I shall never act like a monster. I shall stop eating Fudgie-Fudgies.

I shall always remember this moment, sitting with my father, late at night, at our kitchen table.

I love my father.

Chapter Sixteen

On Friday morning, the day of the night of the Great Eighth Grade Graduation Dance, Emily wakes up with a sore throat and a headache. There are myriad reasons why nobody else in the Conlan family is as expendable (Father's word) today as I am.

Mom feels guilty.

"Don't feel guilty," I tell her.

(I'm delighted to stay home from school, take care of my little sister, and be spared any association with the eighth grade of Holy Redeemer on this, their day of days.)

"Do you have any schoolwork you can do at home?" Mom asks.

"Lots," I tell her, to ease her mind.

"I think Em will be asleep most of the time."

"Don't worry about it."

"If I didn't have a new secretary coming in this morning . . . and if your father didn't have a settlement he must attend . . ."

"Mom," I say, "I won't be missing a thing. It's almost summer. School is almost over."

"Well, practice your piano." she says.

"Okay."

"Softly."

"Okay."

"I still feel guilty."

One by one, the family cars pull out of the Conlan driveway: Fath's, Mary Lou's, Mom's, Michael's.

"The Conlans are coming, o-ho, o-ho. . . ." sings Michael. He's in his Friday mood: date night, Amy.

At last my noisy family is gone.

I look in on Emily. She sleeps. I tiptoe downstairs and play the piano, softly. I don't practice exercises, which I should do. I play "I'm Poor Little Buttercup." I play "Tit-Willow." I go upstairs and peek into Emily's room. Emily wakes up. I take her temperature. It's normal.

"You're supposed to read me a story," she says.

"First," I tell her, "I'm supposed to call Mom."

When I ask for Mom at her office, she's on the line so fast I know she's been anxious for my call. I tell her Emily is doing fine. When I return to read to Em, she has fallen back asleep, so I go downstairs.

The house, with screened doors and windows open to the warm day, is airy and cool and full of odd little creaks and settlings as though, with so many Conlans gone, it can relax and rest itself. I love to be alone in it.

In the kitchen I open a container of vanilla yogurt and mix in a little cherry Kool-Aid. I take this outside and sit on our back steps in the sunshine, with Waldo beside me.

Mom's purple irises are in bloom along the low stone wall that divides our property from Buckleys' over on Harvey Street, and her bed of pink and white peonies is swelling into flower. Two crows chase one another, scolding, into Schultzes' chestnut tree and are quiet. From everywhere comes the warm, sweet, piercing scent of summer. Happiness overwhelms me.

"The flowers appear on the earth," I whisper. *"The time of the singing of birds is come, and the voice of the turtle is heard in our land. . . ."*

Then I think of Cara.

My heart breaks.

Chapter Seventeen

It is Friday evening, and Michael is whistling while getting ready for his carnival date with Amy.

Mary Lou is humming while getting ready for her movie date with Johnnie.

The whole upstairs of the Conlan house reeks of Michael's after-shave lotion and Mary Lou's perfume.

Jennifer, who is going NOWHERE this evening, is being deafened by the buzz of Michael's electric razor, the click of Mary Lou's high heel shoes, and all the whistling and humming.

Jennifer, who is going NOWHERE this evening, will be glad when Michael and Mary Lou leave, and there is peace and quiet.

Michael taps on Jennifer's bedroom door. "Sure you don't want to come with Amy and me?" he asks.

"Michael, I told you. . .!"

"Look," he says, "you helped me out with Amy's flowers. What goes around comes around."

"I do not need help."

"You look lower than a snake's belly," Michael tells me. "And you're pigging out on Fudgie-Fudgies. And you're getting zits!"

"Get out of my room!"

"Zits!" Michael shouts. "Zits! Zits! ZITS!"

"Michael, get . . . OUUUUUUT!"

"What's going on up there?" Father shouts.

"Mom!" Emily wails. "Mom. . . !"

"Ted!" Mom shouts. "You've wakened Emily!"

"Quiet!" shouts Mary Lou. "What will Johnnie think?"

"Johnnie's here!" shouts Robert.

So much for Dear Denise.

Chapter Eighteen

It's hot up here in the attic. Our air conditioning doesn't make it up this far. I don't care, because I don't much like air conditioning. I don't like screens in windows, either. So, after Michael stomps back down the stairs, I slip my screen out and lean it against the wall. Then I turn out the light and curl up on the floor.

It's beginning to get dark. In Schultzes' chestnut tree, birds are twittering, settling down. I love that sound! No matter how bad I may ever feel in my entire life, I know I'll always be grateful that I have ears to hear that sound.

I can see a sliver of moon now, tipped down, a spill-water moon, turning gold, and a light has just gone on upstairs at Larsons' house, across the street. When a car turns the corner of Harvey and Greenwood, its headlights sweep the darkness from a row of maple trees. Then darkness swallows them up again.

By this time lights will be on in Holy Redeemer's church hall, too. Kids will be going in: J.J. Hernandez, Brandon Ackerman, Sharon Riley, Cara. . . . I'm probably the only eighth grader not there.

A tap on my door. It's my mom. She doesn't ask why my light is off. She doesn't say, Jennifer, why are you sitting here in the dark?

I love my mom.

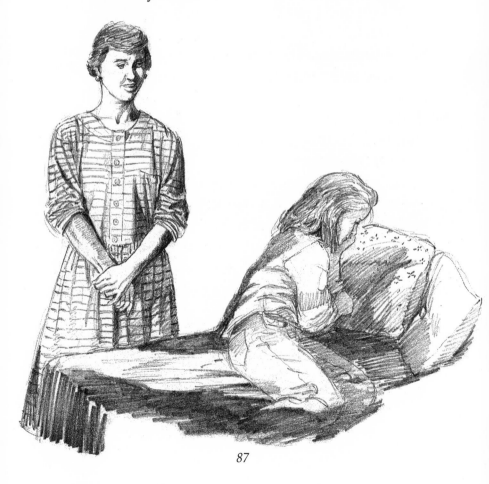

"Emily is longing for orange sherbet," she says. "And Dolly and Sam Flannery have just dropped in downstairs. Would you go to King's for me? And take Robert along? With Em sick, he's at loose ends."

Robert and I head off for King's Deli.

Inside a house on Franklin Street, as we pass by, a woman sits under a lamp reading a newspaper. Newspapers remind me of Brandon, who else?

Robert says, "Mom said I could get a chocolate soda, y' know."

I tell him I know.

We walk along, sometimes in dense blackness under the branches of trees thick with leaves, sometimes in a circle of light from a street lamp. Our sneakers hit the pavement in perfect step: *pad, pad.* Now and then, a car tools by. After it passes, our footsteps sound again: *pad, pad.*

We don't talk until we're almost at King's Deli. Then Robert says, "Jennifer, I'm sorry about your graduation dance."

Chapter Nineteen

When Robert and I push through the door at King's Deli, I find out I'm *not* the only eighth grader not at my graduation dance, because there sitting on a stool at the soda fountain, drinking a large something or other and looking right at me when I walk in, is—

LAWRENCE RIMMER!

Lawrence, who takes his piano lesson right after I take mine at Alison Houston's house.

Lawrence, who walked in the door and found Alison and Toddie and me all screaming into each others' faces.

So here is Lawrence, sitting at the soda fountain, and here am I, happy to find another eighth grader who isn't at the Great Eighth Grade Graduation Dance.

I smile at Lawrence.

Lawrence does NOT smile back.

Robert marches up to the counter and sits down beside Lawrence. I sit down beside Robert, where else?

"Hi!" I say to Lawrence, over Robert's head.

Lawrence frowns. "Hi."

Such enthusiasm, I say to myself.

To the waitress behind the counter, Robert says, "I'd like a chocolate soda with vanilla ice cream."

To the waitress, I say, "I'll pick up a pint of orange sherbet on my way out."

I look at Lawrence. "So . . . ," I say, encouragingly.

Lawrence is concentrating on his drink. In fact, he seems to be choking on it. Or could it be the sight of me that he's choking on?

But what did I ever do to Lawrence Rimmer to deserve this? Surely, his animosity (Father's word) cannot be directed at trying-to-be-friendly me?

Lawrence rises. He is quite tall. "So long," he says. To Robert.

Robert looks up. "So long."

Lawrence does not look at me. I am puzzled. I am intrigued. What is Lawrence Rimmer's problem?

I say, "Not going to the dance, Lawrence?"

I have caught Lawrence's attention. His eyes are like two fiery coals, burning into mine. (By this I mean that I find Lawrence Rimmer very attractive.)

"I didn't have a date," he tells me.

"Neither," I admit frankly, "did I."

"Oh, no?" he replies. (More accurately, he chews up these words and spits them at me.)

Naturally, I'm surprised. "Uh, no."

On one side of me Robert is guzzling his soda. Lawrence approaches my other side. "Do I

look strange to you?" he murmurs.

"Uh, no."

"Not demented? Deranged? Diabolical?" (Lawrence sounds a little like Father.)

"Uh, not at all."

"Then why didn't you want to go to the dance with me?"

"Whaaat?!"

He starts chewing words again, grinding them between his teeth. "The eighth grade graduation dance. Why didn't you want to go with me?"

He is very upset. Even Robert notices, and stops guzzling.

"Well, uh . . . you didn't ask me?"

"Correct me if I'm wrong (grind, grind). First J.J. Hernandez asks me if I'd like to take you to our graduation dance. I say yes. Then J.J. tells me you say no. Next, Sister Kristie Anne asks me if I'd like to take you to our graduation dance. I say yes. Then I learn that you say no. Next, Alison Houston asks me if I'd like to take you to our graduation dance. I say yes. You say no. And now tonight, you tell me that the reason you are not at our graduation dance is that you *didn't have a date!*"

I close my eyes.

Oh!

Ohhhhh!

Ohhhhhhhhh! No! No!

I open my eyes.

"Lawrence, I didn't know it was you."

"What?!"

"I didn't know the date was you. Nobody told me." (BECAUSE I NEVER ASKED!)

I'm embarrassed.

I'm mortified.

I'm—so—dumb!

"So now what?" Lawrence is saying.

I say, "Huh?"

"It's still early. Do you want to go or what?"

"What?"

"Jennifurrr . . ." It's my brother Robert. He has finished his chocolate soda. He is kibitzing. I have no privacy! "Do you want to go to the dance?"

I turn to him. "Why, Robert, you see, I—eeek! yump! glup! oops! eeek!"

Lawrence says, "Does that mean yes?"

I turn to Lawrence. I smile. "Well, sure. I guess."

Chapter Twenty

The next night is Saturday night. My parents have gone across the street to play cards at the Larsons'. Michael has a date with Amy (naturally). Mary Lou has a date with Johnnie (naturally). I am baby-sitting Emily and Robert.

As soon as they are asleep, I go down to Father's office-away-from-the-office. I open the window by my father's desk and take a deep breath of the soft night air. It smells of earth and flowering trees and springtime. It smells heavenly. I do *not* eat a Fudgie-Fudgie.

I dial the Kemptons', where Cara is baby-sitting.

"Are they asleep?" I ask when she answers, meaning Buster and Penelope, the Kemptons' two little kids.

"Yes," says Cara.

"So what do you think about Lawrence Rimmer?" I say.

Cara doesn't beat around the bush. "I think he really likes you."

"Do you really?"

"Didn't he tell you?"

"Tell me what?"

"That he likes you."

"No, he didn't."

"Well, anyone could tell."

"Oh, Cara, do you really think so?"

"I noticed he had his arm around you a lot of the time last night. When you weren't even dancing, that is. That means he cares."

Streaks shoot through me. "Oh, Cara, thank you for saying that!"

"Well, I really think so."

"Oh, Cara, thank you."

But Cara isn't her old chirpy self. "J.J. likes Rachel Henderson now," she says.

I say, "Oh, Cara, no!"

"He does. He told me so."

"Oh, Cara, no!"

"Jennifer, don't keep saying 'Oh, Cara, no'!"

Cara and I only just made up at the dance, so the last thing I want is to get her mad at me!

"Cara," I say, "I know just how you feel."

"Jennifer, you don't!" Cara shouts into my ear. "Nobody in this whole world can possibly know how I feel!"

"Right!," I say. "*Right!*"

(After all, I can put myself into Cara's shoes and understand this is a time when Cara doesn't want me to put myself into her shoes.)

Dear Denise, Aren't you proud?